To Matt and Patrick Murphy, who taught
me the power of stories.

– M.M.

Thank you, Mr. Giles, for giving me my first
set of markers and the encouragement to
create something magical with them.

– J.H.

www.mascotbooks.com

Lilly Lou Makes a New Friend

For more information, please contact:
Mascot Books
620 Herndon Parkway #320
Herndon, VA 20170
info@mascotbooks.com

Library of Congress Control Number: 2018912033

CPSIA Code: PRT0118A
ISBN-13: 978-1-68401-996-0

Printed in the United States

Lilly Lou Makes a New Friend

by Mike Murphy

illustrations by Jonathan Hoefer

CHAPTER ONE

Lilly Lou Makes a New Friend

Lilly Lou lived on a small farm in a small town in the middle of Missouri.

Lilly Lou had two dogs, three sheep, four cats, five pigs, six chickens, and a milking cow. Every day before school, she helped her father feed the animals and milk Milly Moo, her cow.

After school, Lilly Lou would help her mother feed the animals, collect the eggs, and milk Milly Moo. Mrs. Lou would always give Lilly Lou a chance to get milk out of Milly Moo's udders, but Lilly Lou's hands were not strong enough to get more than a little trickle of milk to come out.

When chores were over, Lilly Lou loved to paint. She painted her animals, she painted the sky, she painted her mother, and she painted her father. Lilly Lou told her parents she wanted to be a painter when she grew up.

One night after the dirty dinner dishes had been washed, dried, and put away, Lilly Lou and her parents were sitting by the fire reading a book about birds when they heard a crash outside of their house.

Mr. Lou told Lilly Lou and her mother to wait inside until he could see what made the crashing noise.

Mr. Lou pulled back the curtains and looked out into the darkness but couldn't see anything. So he put on his jacket, grabbed a flashlight, and ran out the door.

Lilly Lou and her mother pulled back the curtains so they could see. The beam from the flashlight reflected off a huge egg-like capsule sitting right in the middle of their barnyard. Lilly Lou and her mother both pulled on their jackets and ran out into the yard to join Mr. Lou.

"What is it, daddy?" Lilly asked her father. "How did it get here?"

"Just stand back," he told her. "I think I hear something inside."

Everyone listened. It was very quiet, and then the top of the egg-like structure exploded open.

The Lous all jumped back.

"Ouch! That hurt!" exclaimed the blue panda-like creature in a gray spacesuit that was crawling out of the capsule.

"Don't move!" Mr. Lou said, pointing his flashlight at the creature.

"Did that creature just say something?" Mrs. Lou said, more as a statement than a question.

"Yes, I did," said the furry creature. "But I didn't know people could speak. Are you special? Who taught you to speak?"

"Of course people can speak. But what are you and how did you get here?" Lilly Lou asked. Her father had lowered his flashlight, but he held Lilly Lou back from getting too close.

"Me?" the creature said as he flopped out of the spaceship and onto the ground. He brushed some debris off his head and started to stand. "I'm Moozy Toozy from Mooz. You can call me Moozy Toozy."

Unlike a panda, he stood on two feet. He was a little taller than Lilly Lou with blue and gray fur.

The rhyming of his name made Lilly Lou laugh. "Well," she said, "you can call me Lilly Lou and these are my parents."

This made Moozy Toozy laugh.

"What happened? How did you get here? And what is that smell?" Mr. Lou asked.

Moozy Toozy tapped his head and sniffed the air. "I don't know, I don't know, and I don't know." he replied. "One minute my brother Moozy Woozy and I were doing tricks in our new Moozypeds, and the next thing I knew I was flying past all these bright lights until I came to a stop right here. Where am I?"

"You are at our farm in Missouri. Are you friendly? And what is that funny odor?" Lilly Lou asked.

"Yes, and the smell started when we passed the star Zeon," he said softly with a bit of a whimper.

"Will Moozy Woozy or someone else come and get you?" Mrs. Lou asked.

"I don't know. This has never happened to me before," Moozy Toozy said softly, and then he started to cry.

Lilly Lou and her parents had never heard anyone or anything cry like Moozy Toozy.

He cried so loud that the two dogs started to howl. The three sheep bayed, the four cats caterwauled, the five pigs snorted, the six chickens cackled, and Milly Moo started mooing louder than she ever had before.

The noises coming from Moozy Toozy and all the farm animals echoed across the fields. Lilly Lou and her parents could see the lights come on at surrounding farms. Lilly covered her ears, Mr. Lou went to calm down Milly, and Mrs. Lou tried to comfort Moozy Toozy.

Just as Moozy Toozy was starting to quiet down, Mrs. Lou could see that Mr. French, who lived on the farm down the road, was in his truck and heading their way.

"Lilly come help me. We need to hide Moozy Toozy before Mr. French sees him!" Lilly did not question her mother. She grabbed one of Moozy Toozy's fingers and tried to pull him toward the barn. Mrs. Lou grabbed a huge tarp that was by the barn and covered up Moozy Toozy's spaceship.

Just as Mr. French pulled into the driveway, they got Moozy Toozy and his furry

body into the barn with Lilly Lou.

Mrs. Lou closed the barn door and went out into the barnyard and waited for Mr. French.

Mr. French was the nosiest man in the county. When he got out of his truck he asked, "Everything OK, Lucy? Sounds like your animals have seen the devil! Where's Lou and where's Lilly Lou?"

"Everything is fine," Mrs. Lou replied with her fingers crossed behind her back. "They are tending to the animals. Lou's out at the corral with Milly Moo. Why don't you go see how he's doing?"

"Do you know what time it is?" he said with some annoyance in his tone. "I was already asleep when your creatures made enough noise to raise the dead! Wait until the boys at the café hear about this one!"

"Hi Fred," Mr. Lou said as he came from around the barn. "I'll bet all our noise woke you up. Sorry about that, but it sure is nice of you to come check on us. We'd have done the same for you. But everything is calm now. Why don't you go back to bed? Sure do appreciate you coming over."

Mr. Lou was hoping Mr. French would leave, so he started walking toward Mr. French's truck to give him a hint, but Mr. French lifted his nose into the air and sniffed. "What is that funny smell? I don't think I've ever smelled anything like it."

Once again, Mrs. Lou crossed her fingers behind her back and then she said, "Lilly Lou and I were experimenting with some new recipes and while we were cooking, we got distracted with her homework and burnt the casserole to a crisp. It stunk up the whole house. I'm tempted to sleep outside, it's so bad in there! But don't worry about us, Mr. French. The odor is probably what got the animals all riled up. You just go on home. We'll see you soon." Then she turned around and headed toward the barn.

"Strange place you have here, Lou. Boys at the café won't believe this one. Lou Lou's animals having a fit over a burnt casserole! I still think they saw the devil," he mumbled as he got in his truck and drove off.

Mr. Lou waited until the taillights of Mr. French's truck were out of sight and then he ran to the barn. He swung open the barn door and yelled, "Lilly Lou, where are you? Are you OK?"

There was no response. The barn was dark. He remembered putting the flashlight down by the corral. He ran over to get it and then ran back to the barn.

"Where is Lilly Lou?" Mrs. Lou asked. "She didn't answer."

Lilly Lou's parents turned on the flashlight and entered the barn, sweeping the light across the floor of the barn as they went from stall to stall. They were both getting scared when they had not found Lilly Lou, but then they came to the last stall and there she was.

Lilly Lou, Moozy Toozy, two dogs, three sheep, and four cats were all cuddled up in the last stall. They were all asleep. Moozy Toozy had a high-pitched snore that sounded like a beginning band student learning to play an old clarinet.

"I don't think we can leave her here, and I don't know what to do about him," Mr. Lou said.

"Let's see if we can get Lilly Lou up and inside. Then we can figure out what to do with our unusual guest."

Mr. and Mrs. Lou were able to get Lilly Lou into the house and were followed by two dogs and four cats. The three sheep stayed cuddled up next to Moozy Toozy. They put Lilly Lou in her bed and the cats and dogs climbed up to join her. Mr. and Mrs. Lou shut off the lights and went to sit by the fireplace.

"What are we going to do with this Moozy Toozy from Mooz, Lou?" asked Mrs. Lou.

"Let's just sleep on it," he replied. "He seems friendly enough and thankfully, Fred French didn't see him. We can decide what to do in the morning."

CHAPTER TWO

The Plan

Even though it was Saturday, Lilly Lou got up while it was still dark outside, put on her clothes, and went out with her father to feed the farm animals, milk Milly Moo, and check on Moozy Toozy. She grabbed the flashlight from her father and ran into the barn.

"Moozy Toozy, are you here?" she called out.

The unusual odor was still in the air and she heard a high-pitched snore coming from the back stall.

"What is that noise?" she asked her father.

"I'm pretty sure that's coming from Moozy Toozy. He was making the same sound last night when we found you with him."

Lilly Lou and her father walked over to the stall, and there was Moozy Toozy and the three sheep, sound asleep.

"Should we wake him up?" she wondered.

"Let's do our chores first. Then we can come back and see if we can wake him up," her father suggested.

Lilly Lou and her father, Lou, fed the farm animals, milked Milly Moo the cow, and went back to the barn. The sun had come up and the early morning light set the barnyard aglow. Lucy opened the barn door and the sheep bolted out. Moozy Toozy stumbled out behind them and moved his head back and forth as he took in the surroundings.

"This doesn't look anything like Mooz. Where did you say I am?" he asked.

"This is our farm in the middle of Missouri. Your capsule crashed into our barnyard last night. Then you started crying and we hid you in our barn so Mr. French would not see you. Do you remember?" Lilly Lou asked.

"Yes, that was embarrassing. I can't remember crying since I was a little baby. I am worried about Moozy Woozy. I wish I knew where he is! He always gets lost no matter where we go. This is all very strange," Moozy Toozy answered.

"Well, it's time for breakfast. We need to go in. You're welcome to join us," Mr. Lou offered.

They all went into the house where Mrs. Lou had made eggs, bacon, and a stack of pancakes from the World Famous Paddy's Pancake Mix. The two dogs and four cats sniffed and rubbed up against Moozy Toozy. "Wash your hands and come have a seat," she instructed her family.

"Moozy Toozy, I must admit I've never had a guest from Mooz. What do you eat?"

"Moozpops are my favorite food and we all drink lots of Moozjuice, but I'll try anything you are serving. Whenever we go on trips our parents have us eat the food popular with the people we visit," Moozy Toozy replied.

"Where have you been?" all three of the Lous asked in chorus.

"Last year we went to Grand Mooz. The year before that we went to Little Mooz, and the year before that we went to Middle Mooz. They had very odd food there."

"Have you ever been to Earth before?" Lilly Lou asked.

"No. We knew you were here and we knew that creatures like you lived here, but this is my first visit. My parents are probably never going to let me out of our globe again."

"How old are you Moozy Toozy, and what is a globe?" Lilly Lou asked.

Mrs. Lou interrupted the conversation. "The food is going to get cold. Have a pancake Moozy Toozy. Hope you like it."

Moozy Toozy grabbed a few with his hand and stuffed them in his mouth. Then he let out a loud burp.

Lilly Lou giggled and Mr. and Mrs. Lou exchanged a glance and raised their eyebrows.

Moozy Toozy let out another enormous burp and this time they all exploded into laughter! Moozy Toozy laughed along with them, and then he asked for more

pancakes, which Mrs. Lou promptly passed to him. Again, he stuffed them in his mouth, swallowed, and let out a burp that made the two dogs lift their ears.

"So, Moozy Toozy, how old are you, and what do you mean you live in a globe?" Lilly Lou asked again.

"I'm 1,451 Mooz Days old and a globe is like this house but much smaller and we do not have walls on the inside," Moozy Toozy answered.

For the next hour Moozy Toozy and the Lous asked each other questions and gave answers that required more questions. Lilly Lou was drawing paintings of Moozy Toozy and handing them to him and her parents. Moozy Toozy broke into a huge smile.

"What do you call this?" he asked.

"It's a painting. Do you paint on Mooz?" Lilly Lou replied and added her own question.

"No," he answered. "I would like to try but first, I must go find Moozy Woozy. I sure hope he is OK!"

"Can we help?" Lilly Lou asked.

"I don't know, but you can certainly come along."

"How do you plan to start your search? What does Moozy Woozy look like?" Mr. Lou asked.

"He looks just like me with beautiful green fur all over his body. He was a model when we were babies," Moozy Toozy replied.

Then, Moozy Toozy scratched his head and walked out the door. The Lous followed him. He went over to the capsule and pulled the tarp off and climbed inside. All the Lous stuck their heads in to see what he was doing. A few minutes later Moozy Toozy crawled out of the capsule and was holding a shiny ball. He held it up toward the sky and said, "Moozy Woozy, are you out there?"

A few seconds passed, and then a scratchy voice started coming from the ball. "Yes, I'm here. I'm in some place called New York. My Moozyped flopped into this river. There is a big statue of a lady holding up a torch and I'm surrounded by these tall buildings. I've never seen anything like it! Where are you?" Moozy Woozy asked.

"I'm on a farm in Missouri with the Lous. How can I get to you?"

"Ask the Lous. I'm sure you remember that I've never been here or there before," Moozy Woozy replied with a touch of sarcasm in his voice.

"How do we get to New York?" Moozy Toozy asked the Lous.

"We studied driving distances in Social Studies. I just happen to know that we are 1,068 miles from NYC. We can drive there in 16 hours. Mom and Dad can take turns driving and we will be there by late tomorrow!" Lilly Lou exclaimed with complete confidence.

"We can't do that!" Mr. Lou barked. "Who will take care of the animals and milk Milly Moo?"

"Well," Mrs. Lou said, "we could tell Mr. French that we have to attend very special and private family business and ask him to watch over the animals for two days. We could drive there, find Moozy Woozy, connect him with Moozy Toozy, and then drive back. I think Mr. French would do that for us if we can stand having him snoop all around our farm for two days."

"I've never been to New York!" Lilly Lou exclaimed with excitement. "That sounds like a great plan. Can we do it Daddy? Please ask Mr. French to watch our animals. I've always wanted to see New York! Just imagine, me at the Statue of Liberty! Me at the Empire State Building! Me at Carnegie Hall! Me at the Metropolitan Museum of Art! What do you think, Moozy Toozy?"

"I wish my Moozyped was working, but that sounds better than nothing. Would you do all that travel just for me?"

"Let me see what Mr. French says," Mr. Lou replied. Then he got in his truck and took off down the lane.

Fifteen minutes later, Lilly Lou, her mother, and Moozy Toozy could see the truck returning down the lane with a cloud of dust coming from behind.

Mr. Lou jumped out of the truck and exclaimed, "He said he would do it! Everyone go get what you need. We will leave in 30 minutes. Moozy Toozy, Lilly Lou, Lucy Lou, we are going to New York City!"

Everyone cheered and then ran to get their things for the trip. Twenty-five minutes later, five minutes ahead of time, they were heading down the lane on their way to New York City to reunite Moozy Toozy with Moozy Woozy.

CHAPTER THREE

Off to New York

Mr. and Mrs. Lou were in the front seat and Lilly Lou and Moozy Toozy were in the back. "Buckle up," Mr. Lou ordered and he started down the lane. Just before he reached the road, he jammed on the brakes, thrusting everyone forward and sending up a cloud of dust that shrouded the truck. "Moozy's space capsule! We forgot to hide it. We can't let Mr. French find it!" Mr. Lou exclaimed.

So back they went. Lilly Lou wanted to hide it in the hay loft. Mrs. Lou wanted to bury it. Mr. Lou wanted to hide it in the woods, but they finally agreed with Moozy Toozy to load it in the back of a hay wagon and cover it with the tarp. They were all surprised how light Moozy Toozy's space capsule weighed. Once they had it secured and covered in the back of the wagon, they pushed it to the back of the barn. Then they jumped back into the truck and headed down the lane and due east to New York City.

The trip to New York was mostly uneventful. Mr. Lou would drive for three hours, then Mrs. Lou would drive for three. Lilly Lou and Moozy Toozy played games with Lilly's dolls and action figures. Lilly Lou did some drawing and let Moozy Toozy try, but the pens and crayons did not fit well in his furry paws. The only excitement was when Moozy Toozy convinced the Lous to let him drive.

He was the only person in the car who had ever driven in outer space. What could be so hard about driving a pick-up?

Moozy Toozy was amazed to learn that earth cars could not go up or down to get around another vehicle. After almost running into the back of three cars in Ohio, Mr. Lou decided Moozy Toozy needed to stick to space travel and let the Lous manage driving on earth.

As Lilly Lou had stated, the group entered the city limits of New York City exactly 16 hours and 1,068 miles from their start at the farm. Both Lilly Lou and Moozy Toozy stuck their heads out the windows. Lilly Lou kept repeating, "Look at that building! Look at how tall that one is! That one is even taller! Are we at the Empire State Building yet? Did you know the Empire State Building was built in 1931 and is 103 stories tall?"

Moozy Toozy kept yelling for his brother. "Moozy Woozy where are you? Answer me! We are coming, brother!"

Mr. Lou used his GPS to find the Statue of Liberty. When he parked the truck, Lilly Lou jumped out and ran up to every person she saw, telling him or her that the statue was the Statue of Liberty.

"Look," she exclaimed, "that is the Statue of Liberty! Frederic Auguste Bartholdi, a Frenchman, sculpted and dedicated the statue in 1886. It was a gift from the people of France to the United States. The lady is the Roman goddess of freedom, Libertas. Isn't she beautiful!"

People were impressed with her knowledge and enthusiasm until they saw

Moozy Toozy, who still looked like the blue and gray panda-like creature who had crashed into the Lou's barnyard. The site of the Moozy caught the people by surprise. Moozy was now yelling at the top of his lungs for Moozy Woozy. "Moozy Woozy, I'm here! Where are you, brother? Where are you?"

Some people stopped to take pictures, but many people ran away. The National Park Service Staff approached Lilly Lou. "Miss," the huge uniformed officer who was clearly confused by what he was seeing, said, "is this your dog? Is he talking? He must be on a leash. Is that dog talking?"

"He's Moozy Toozy from Mooz. His Moozyped malfunctioned and he crashed in our barnyard in Missouri. His brother, Moozy Woozy, crashed by the Statue of Liberty. Can you take us there?" Lilly Lou asked.

The officer pulled out a phone and spoke into it. In the meantime, Mr. and Mrs. Lou joined Moozy Toozy and Lilly Lou by the officer. Within minutes, sirens were sounding all around the Statue of Liberty ticket booth and boarding area. Dozens of police and park officers surrounded Moozy Toozy, Lilly Lou, and her parents. Some of the officers had drawn their guns. Others were taking photos, and still others had closed in and were telling the Lous and Moozy Toozy to get on their knees. Mr. Lou tried to protest, but there was too much commotion for anyone to hear him.

Just as the police had started to get everyone quieted down, there was a huge commotion that erupted over at Ellis Island. Somehow Moozy Woozy spotted his brother, and now he was yelling his brother's name as loud as he could. "Moozy Toozy, you came! I'm over here with the big statue and all these people who keep pointing machines that flash in my face. Help me!"

By then, television crews, newspaper reporters, and other media people had arrived and were filming every move. When Moozy Toozy heard his brother's voice, he jumped to his feet, ran to the edge of the boarding area, and bellowed, "I'm over here, brother! We're coming!"

"Don't shoot!" an officer yelled at the policemen who had their guns pointed at Moozy Toozy. "Put your guns away! Give me time to sort this out! Put those weapons away!" he yelled. The policemen slowly but surely followed his directions.

"Now," the officer commanded. He pointed at the Lous. "Let those people get up. I need to hear what is going on."

Lilly Lou jumped to her feet. "I am Lilly Lou and these are my parents, Lou Lou and Lucy Lou. This," she pointed at Moozy Toozy, "is Moozy Toozy. He is from Mooz. He landed in our barnyard last night and we came to New York City to find his brother. He must be that bright green and white furry creature out with Lady Liberty. Can you take us to him?"

Mr. Lou stepped up and said, "That's right, officer. Lilly Lou has told you all we know. I can tell you that Moozy Toozy has not caused any trouble. Granted, he doesn't look like us, but he speaks just as well as any human I have ever met."

Some of the news reporters had their microphones and cameras on the Lous. Others had moved over to Moozy Toozy and were asking him questions. He was so excited to see his brother he kept repeating over and over, "I want to go see Moozy Woozy. I want to go see Moozy Woozy."

The park officers and police moved the Lous over to Moozy Toozy and loaded them on a boat for the short trip over to Ellis Island. When Moozy Toozy and Moozy Woozy were reunited, they rubbed their noses together and gave each other great big Mooz hugs.

Tourists and reporters had pushed the Lous out of the way and were anxiously taking photos and shouting questions at the two Moozites. Moozy Toozy got everyone to quiet down and then said, "I am Moozy Toozy, and this is my brother, Moozy Woozy. We are from Mooz and our Moozypeds have crashed on this planet. That nice family," he pointed at the Lous, "have helped reunite us. Now I ask that you let me introduce my brother to my new friends and then we will answer your questions."

The crowd parted and the Lous were able to walk to the center of the mass of reporters and tourists who were now surrounding the Moozites. Moozy Toozy made the introductions while cameramen were frantically trying to get the best angles of the hugs and handshakes that were taking place.

Then an announcement blared out of a loudspeaker. "Ladies and gentlemen, I am the park service director, and I am going to ask you all to move to the boat landing areas until the park service can get better control of this situation."

Park service officers and police moved everyone except the Lous and the Moozites over to the loading area. The Lous and the Moozites were moved to a boat on the other side of the island and quickly loaded up and taken back to the mainland of New York City.

A reporter saw the boat taking Moozy Toozy, his brother Moozy Woozy, and the Lous away and started yelling for them to stop. But the captain had no

intentions of doing anything but following his orders.

By the time the boat carrying the Moozites and the Lous got back to the main staging area for the trip to the Statue of Liberty, there were dozens of police holding back hundreds of onlookers who had come to see the visitors from outer space. SWAT vans, police cars, and black limousines lined the streets. As soon as the boat docked, the Lous were put in one limo and Moozy Toozy and Moozy Woozy in another. Police cars with sirens blaring and lights flashing led them through the crowd and into the streets of New York.

"This is the most exciting day of my life!" Lilly Lou said to her parents. "We are in a limo in New York City, just like in the movies!"

"Same for me," replied Mrs. Lou. "Wait until Mr. French hears about this. He will have stories for the boys at the café for years to come." They all laughed.

"Where are you taking us?" Mr. Lou asked the huge man who was driving the car.

"We are going to the mayor's office. She wants to meet you and your friends."

"The mayor's office? That sounds interesting, but I want to see the Empire State Building," Lilly Lou replied.

"Well, I'm sure the mayor will be able to arrange a special visit for you. Just ask her," the driver advised.

Meanwhile, in the other limo, officials from the CIA, FBI, and NASA were questioning Moozy Toozy and Moozy Woozy. The scientists from NASA were trying to learn about Mooz and how the space visitors got to Earth. The FBI and CIA were trying to learn why they had come here in the first place. Moozy Toozy was doing his best to answer their questions, and Moozy Woozy kept asking, "When can we go home? I don't like being lost."

Just like at the docks, when the limos reached City Hall, policemen held back crowds of reporters and onlookers. Helicopters flew overhead, and it was difficult for Lilly Lou and her parents to hear what everyone was yelling as they emerged from the vehicle and were rushed into the building. Moozy Toozy, his brother, and the officials from CIA, FBI, and NASA were right behind them.

They were taken to a huge room and asked to have a seat. Men and women came in and offered drinks to everyone, and then the mayor entered. Staff members, including the Chief of Police, surrounded her.

The mayor introduced herself to Moozy Toozy, Moozy Woozy and the Lous and then asked everyone to be seated. She welcomed them all to New York City and then for the next hour let various people take turns asking questions. All of the questions were directed to the Moozites. After an hour or so, the mayor asked the Lous if they had anything they wanted to say.

Mr. and Mrs. Lou told the mayor what had happened at the farm. The mayor then turned to Lilly Lou and asked, "And how about you, little girl, do you have anything you would like to say?"

"The man in the car said I could ask you to take us to the Empire State Building. I would also like to see Carnegie Hall and the Metropolitan Museum of Art, and if you don't mind, I am really hungry. Could we get something to eat?"

"Well," the mayor replied, "I have forgotten my manners." She turned to her staff and said, "Please have Donatello's bring in food for everyone. We can eat in the conference room. Then we will take Miss Lilly Lou and her family on a grand tour of NYC!"

"But what about Moozy Toozy and his brother? What are we going to do to help them?" she asked.

"I want to go back to Mooz," Moozy Woozy whimpered.

"I've got an idea," Moozy Toozy replied. "But we will need to go to the highest place around here to test my plan."

"That's the Empire State Building!" Lilly Lou blurted out. "You can come with us!"

"OK," said the mayor. "First we'll have lunch and then we will all head to the Empire State Building. Now let's head to the conference room. We can continue our conversation there."

While walking to the conference room, Lilly Lou grabbed Moozy Toozy by one of his hands and pulled him over to the side. She whispered into his ear, "If your plan works, will we ever see you again?"

"I don't know," he whispered back. "We are not exactly sure how we got here and are not sure our plan will work."

"If your plan does work, promise me you will try to come back. I like having you as a friend," she replied.

"I'll try," Moozy Toozy said. Then he gave her a big hug and moved on with the others.

CHAPTER FOUR

On Top of the World

"What is that? What is that? What is that?" Lilly Lou bombarded the mayor and her staff with questions.

"Lilly Lou, you have more questions than the entire press corps on election night!" the mayor told her.

The group had moved to the viewing area at the top of the Empire State Building. It was a perfectly clear afternoon and they could all see across the city and into Connecticut, New Jersey, New York, and Pennsylvania.

While the Lous and the mayor were sightseeing, Moozy Toozy, Moozy Woozy, and the officials from NASA were discussing the plan to return the Moozites to Mooz.

"I'm pretty sure that if we can be left alone this evening, we will be able to make contact with our parents," Moozy Toozy shared with the group.

"We will make those arrangements," the mayor replied. "Is there any chance you might return? I am sure our scientists could learn a great deal from you."

"Yes," Dr. Novak, the NASA officer, replied. "We would love to host you and your scientists for an exchange of information about our planets."

"Well, first our plan has to work. If we succeed, we will try to return. You have all been very kind," Moozy Toozy replied.

"So if we are going to stay here, where are we going to go?" Lilly Lou asked.

"Oh, we will spend the night in New York and then come back in the morning to see if the plan worked," Mr. Lou responded.

The mayor asked, "Do you have a place to stay? The city of New York will be pleased to put you up in one of our special guest hotels. We will get you a room at the Plaza. You will love the views. That is the least we can do for your valiant efforts to support our visitors from Mooz. And I think you said something about wanting to see Carnegie Hall? A driver will pick you up at your hotel at seven. He will have tickets for you and will return you to your hotel after the concert."

Lilly Lou gave the mayor a hug. "Thank you! Thank you! Thank you, Madam Mayor!"

"That would be very nice, your Honor," Mrs. Lou chimed in.

The group said their farewells to Moozy Toozy and Moozy Woozy and headed out. Lilly Lou hugged the two Moozites and gave Moozy Toozy a kiss on his head. "Be careful and try to come back," she whispered in his ear.

The mayor had a driver take the Lous to the Plaza Hotel adjacent to Central Park. While moving through the streets, the driver explained that the Plaza was one of the most famous hotels in the world. "Kings, queens, and presidents have stayed at the Plaza," the driver explained. "Did you know that the movies *The Great Gatsby*, *The Way We Were*, *Funny Girl*, *Crocodile Dundee*, and of course, *Home Alone*, were filmed in the Plaza?"

"I loved that movie," Lilly giggled her reply.

Lilly Lou and her parents enjoyed their evening at Carnegie Hall, but as they were going back to the Plaza Hotel, Mr. Lou stated that no matter what happened, they needed to start driving back to the farm the next day. "We can't ask Mr. French to spend another day tending to our animals. We have done all we can do here."

By then Lilly Lou was sound asleep. Mr. Lou carried her up to the room. They all slept soundly until the phone started ringing.

"What time is it? Who is this?" Mr. Lou yawned into the phone.

"Mr. Lou, this is the mayor. Did I wake you? I apologize, but I thought you would want to know that when my aides went to check on the Moozites this morning, they were gone. Radar over the city did not show any unusual activity last night so we have no idea where they are. I hope you had a nice evening."

"Yes, yes, your Honor. We all had a delightful time. Thank you for the wonderful hotel and fabulous night at Carnegie Hall. We all had a great time and Lilly Lou loved the performance. She will be excited to hear that Moozy Toozy and Moozy Woozy are on their way home. Goodbye."

Mr. Lou woke up Lilly and Mrs. Lou and told them what the mayor had shared with him. Just then there was a knock on their door. "Room service," a friendly voice sang.

Mr. Lou opened the door and there was a young man with a cart filled with all kinds of food. "Compliments of the mayor," he said. "Oh, and I brought up a few copies of the *Times*. We thought you might like to see the front page."

There on the front page of the *New York Times* was Lilly Lou, Moozy Toozy, Moozy Woozy, and the mayor.

"Wait until Mr. French and the boys at the diner see this!" chuckled Mr. Lou. Mrs. Lou and Lilly laughed along with him.

Lilly sat by the window and looked out onto Central Park at the horses and carriages that were lining up to give tourists a ride through the park.

"Daddy, Mommy," Lilly chirped. "Could we go visit Central Park? Did you know it is almost as big as our farm? There are 842 acres, and it has been named a National Historic Landmark. And see the carriages down there? Some people want to close down the business because they say not all the horses are treated well. Can we please take a short walk?"

Lilly Lou's parents agreed. They ate the delicious breakfast the mayor had sent,

packed up, and then spent an hour visiting Central Park. Just as they were ending their walk, Lilly spotted a horse that looked sick. She went up to the horse to give him an apple, but a big man with a long beard yelled at her to get away before she got trampled.

Lilly looked at her parents and then at the man. "You must be one of the owners who does not take care of your horse. I hope they shut you down. No horse should be mistreated like this."

"What do you know about horses, girly?" the man snarled.

"More than you will ever know," Mr. Lou replied and they all walked away.

CHAPTER FIVE

Home

The trip back to Missouri flew by as the Lous exchanged stories about the incredible adventure with Moozy Toozy and their amazing trip to New York. Mr. Lou called Mr. French when they had traveled halfway back to Missouri and was sure they would get home that night. He thanked Mr. French over and over for watching over the farm and promised to tell him their story once they got home.

Lilly Lou never stopped making drawings of the Statue of Liberty, the Empire State

Building, the Metropolitan Museum of Art, Carnegie Hall, and the Moozites. Her favorite picture was a drawing of Moozy Toozy, Moozy Woozy, her parents, and the mayor standing on the observation deck of the Empire State Building. Her parents said they would get it framed for her.

It was past 3 a.m. when the Lous finally got home. Lilly Lou and her mother carried their bags into the house while Mr. Lou checked the animals. Everything was fine except the Moozyped was gone from the back of the hay wagon. "I'll worry about that in the morning," he said to himself.

Since Lilly Lou had missed a day of school, her mother took her in on Tuesday to make sure the principal, Mr. Gold, did not think Lilly Lou was making up a tall tale. The children were excited to hear Lilly Lou's story about Moozy Toozy and New York.

Later that evening when Lilly Lou got home from school, her mother received a phone call from Mrs. McGolden asking Mrs. Lou to teach Lilly Lou not to tell lies at school.

"What lies is Lilly Lou telling at school?" she asked.

"She told the children that space monsters had landed at your farm and took you to New York. She scared the death out of Sarah Jean. She probably won't sleep tonight because of those lies. Teach your daughter that lies can cause trouble!" Mrs. McGolden screeched.

"Mrs. McGolden, I'm not sure what Lilly Lou told the children at school, but I suggest you take Sarah Jean to get her hearing checked. I'm pretty sure she heard Lilly Lou talk about creatures from space and New York but not the way you relayed the story. There is nothing to worry about. The space creatures were friendly and they have gone home. And if you ever get a chance to go to New York, be sure to visit the Empire State Building and the Statue of Liberty. They are beautiful. Goodbye," Mrs. Lou said with a charming but sarcastic tone. She hung up the phone and wondered why Principal Gold had not told Mrs. McGolden about Lilly Lou's trip.

"Who was that, Mom?" Lilly Lou asked.

Mrs. Lou crossed her fingers behind her back and replied, "One of those reporters from New York. It was nothing."

Two weeks later, everyone was back into their routines.

Lilly Lou had finished her chores and her homework and was painting a map of New York City when she heard something tapping on her window. She looked out and there he was.

Moozy Toozy had kept his promise.

He was back, and he wasn't alone.

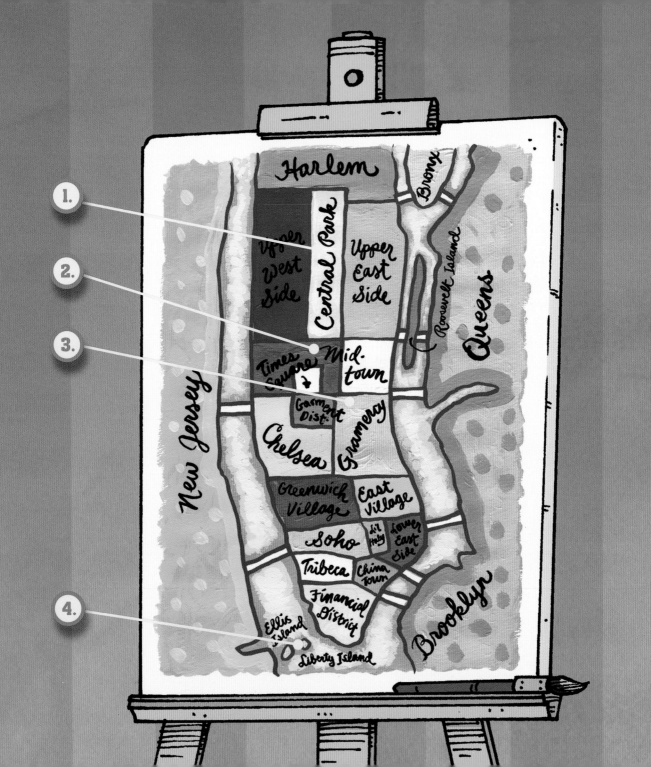

1. Central Park

Central Park is an 842-acre green space in the heart of New York City. Walking paths, lakes, gardens, art, and other attractions make it the most visited and used park in America. It is a National Historic Landmark and as Lilly Lou knows is a well-known location for horse-drawn carriage rides.

2. Carnegie Hall

Carnegie Hall in midtown Manhattan was built in 1891 and has 3,671 seats. It is one of the most prestigious venues in the world for classical and popular music performances.

3. Empire State Building

The Empire State Building is one of the tallest buildings in New York and the world. It was completed in 1931 and is 1,454 feet tall. It has been in over 250 movies and TV shows, including *King Kong*.

4. The Statue of Liberty

The Statue of Liberty is a gift from the people of France to the United States. Sculpted in 1886 by Frédéric Auguste Bartholdi, the lady is the Roman goddess of freedom. The statue holds a prominent position in New York Harbor and has been a symbol of the freedom of America to decades of immigrants and visitors.

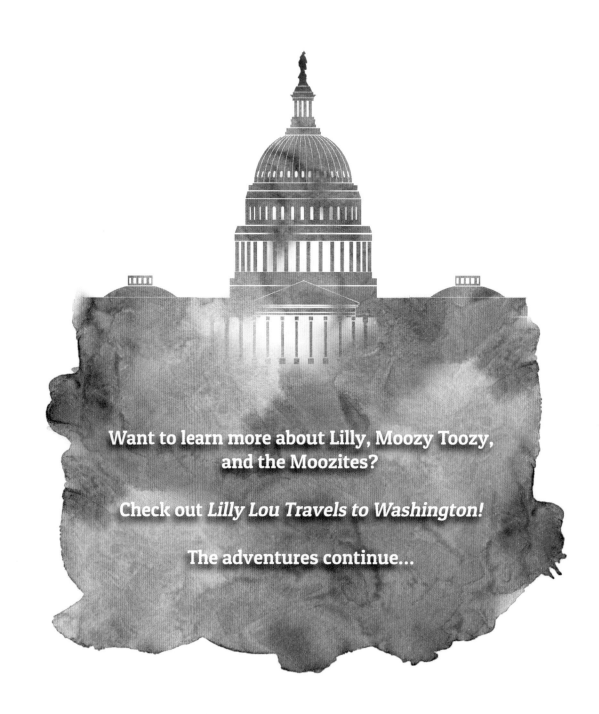

Want to learn more about Lilly, Moozy Toozy,
and the Moozites?

Check out *Lilly Lou Travels to Washington!*

The adventures continue...

Mike Murphy

Mike is a life-long educator and headmaster at Shorecrest Preparatory School, who lives with his wife Robin in St. Petersburg, Florida. When not at school, Mike likes to explore mountains and cities, always with an eye out for birds and interesting people.

Jonathan Hoefer

Jonathan has been drawing for as long as he can remember. A graduate from the illustration program at Syracuse University, he currently lives in Florida with his family.